WEEKLY WAKE

First Published 2022 by Michael and Samaria Sylvester

ISBN: 978-0-578-28633-4

SYLVESTER

WEEKLY WAKE

ACKNOWLEDGMENTS

We dedicate this book to our greatest supporters. Thank you, mom and dad, for being the first to show us creativity, Kelley, and Paulina, for your motivation and non-stop push to be greater. This one's for mom, dad, the Kelster, and the Paulina girl.

CONTENTS

A NOTE FROM THE AUTHORS

With immense joy, we introduce our collection of short stories, *Weekly Wake*. We believe that interest and entertainment lie at the heart of fiction. And that the conventions we follow and the worlds we build point towards a truth we believe in. Packed into this book lie our unique sense of humor, experience with friendship, family, and flying on planes. We hope you enjoy, relate, and immerse yourself in our vivid imagination. That it entertains is a given, that it prompts thoughtful exploration and creativity, is our desire.

WEEKLY WAKE

Aspen woke up delighted and determined to have the best day. She took a hot shower, then searched her closet for something pretty. Her eyes shot towards an unfamiliar pink garment bag tucked in between her dresses. She slid the plastic off the hanger to discover a brand-new dress! Most likely a gift from her mother for the new season. The babydoll dress was hemmed with ruffles and tied at the shoulders with satin ribbons. The dress fell just above the knee and beautifully flattered her youthful figure. Aspen smiled contently as she viewed herself in the mirror.

"Aspen, honey, are you ready?" Nick called out from downstairs.

His voice shook her out of her thoughts. Aspen jumped into a familiar pair of black loafers and raced down the staircase. Waiting at the bottom of the steps was her father. Nick stood tall and slender at six feet and two inches. He wore a dark button-up shirt tucked into perfectly pressed black slacks. She swung happily into his arms, hoping he would notice her new dress.

"You look beautiful. Is that a new dress?"

Nick fondled the ribbons tied on her shoulders. Aspen smiled wildly. Nick and Aspen had a special relationship that could rival any father-daughter duo. While there was room in his heart for both daughters, he was particularly close with Aspen as her deep brown curls resembled his wife's hair. She was the spitting image of her mom.

"Yes, Mom bought it just for today."

"Just for today? Well, we better get going then!"

Nick scooped her up and carried her over his shoulder. Her mother, Alice, and sister, Riley, were waiting in a black sedan. Once settled in the back seat, Aspen couldn't help but smile. Mom wore her vintage satin collar necklace with the matching black bracelet. The exact same collar Cinderella had worn in the princess movie. Her dad had promised to buy her the same set when she turned sixteen. She looked towards her sister to compare outfits, who was dressed in a pleated skirt and her go-to turtleneck. Aspen hated that turtleneck. It was like a drawn-out friendship; it fit poorly and only worked because it was comfortable. Although not half as fabulous as herself, she decided that Riley looked sufficiently pretty. The whole family seemed to glow in their signature shade of black.

The Grays held a unique tradition that kept them close. While some families spent their weekends at the beach or the zoo, the Grays shared their Saturdays at a new service each week. The tradition gave each member time to reflect, re-center, and refuel. As they pulled up to the church, excitement snowballed in Aspen. Her eyes gleamed at the packed parking lot. There was an orange vested man directing traffic. The larger the crowd, the easier it was to blend in. Once parked, Nick turned to the back seat to review the rules.

"Girls, remember to separate and remain unnoticed."

Riley and Aspen both nodded before rushing out of the car. They were anxious to get a seat near the altar. Ignoring their father's instructions, they sat together in the front. Aspen glanced down her row and viewed a sea of pale cheeks and cold frowns. She squealed. Once the rest of the attendees were seated, a stout man stepped onto the platform and gripped the podium. He greeted the room with sympathetic eyes and spoke in a somber tone.

"We are gathered here today to say goodbye to our great friend, Robert Daniels. He was an excellent provider, loyal husband, and a proud assistant manager at J.J.'s Discounts for thirty years. Some say it was his dedication to his job that led him to an early passing, but only God knows why this wonderful man was taken from us at such a young age."

The bereaved family was propped up, seated on the left side of the pulpit. The nephew of the deceased, around eight years old, was picking at a scar on his arm while another relative, a few years older, had his head bowed in deep concentration. What appeared to be him grieving was actually him deciding between thick or thin crust for his mobile order. Next to the boys sat Mrs. Daniels, who was sincerely miserable. Having lost a piece of her heart, she felt threatening loneliness creep inside. She had never met anyone like her husband and was afraid she never would again. Mrs. Daniels approached the mic with heavy steps and had words: "To know him was to love him. He had a magical way of making you feel seen and understood. He entered every conversation not to educate but to learn and to be amazed. He was a man that loved through action. He didn't always say, 'I love you,' but I heard it every time he paused his world to save mine. He was always patient, selfless, and seemed to exist to make me happy. I understand that no one can live forever, but…." Mrs. Daniels struggled to continue her speech and let out a soft cry. Another relative gently escorted her back to her seat.

"She's such an ugly crier," Riley said loud enough for the rows behind her to hear. Whispers floated around, and people shot disapproving glares at the two girls.

"Excuse me," whispered an elderly woman seated behind. "How exactly are you two related to Mr. Daniels?"

This was the family's favorite question. At some point at every funeral, they'd be asked how they knew the deceased family member. This was the highlight of their Weekly Wake, the glorious opportunity to make an impression on people they'd never meet again. The familiar question was asked so often, the girls had a different answer each time. Sometimes they were church members, former students, or distant relatives. Last week, Nick told the deceased man's father that he was an old childhood friend. Having met very few of his son's friends, the father asked Nick to have words. After muddling through a shockingly eloquent and riveting speech, the crowd was deeply moved.

Caught off-guard by the woman's question, Riley nervously looked to Aspen for an answer.

Aspen expertly lied in a discreet whisper, "We're his children from a previous marriage."

Riley gave Aspen a smirk of approval for successfully disturbing the woman.

Towards the end of the funeral, everyone lined up at the altar to view the coffin. Riley's excitement could not be contained. Aspen sighed as she witnessed Riley pulling out her phone. Once the girls advanced to the front of the line, Riley leaned over the man's remains and attempted to take a selfie with Mr. Daniel's corpse. At the glare of the flash, all eyes shot towards Riley. From the back of the line, Nick and his wife quickly realized their daughters had attracted attention.

"Crap! It's blurry. Aspen, you made me rush… It's your fault!"

Riley fussed over her shot of the body, utterly unbothered by the attention.

"What do you think you're doing?" a deeply offended stranger asked.

"Don't worry. I'll edit the photo before I post it. Ya know, give him a little more color," Riley snarked.

Aspen pulled on Riley's arm. "Just put your phone away. You're causing a scene."

"I know, I just need to get one more shot...."

Riley tilted her phone for a better angle. Leaning too far in, she lost her grip. Riley immediately fished the phone from the coffin and retreated to her sister's side. She looked behind her to see if anyone had noticed her fumble. Her eyes met several angry faces—two of them being her parents. Nick loudly cleared his throat. And the girls knew it was time to leave.

"Riley! I told you not to draw attention. What were you thinking?" He took a breath to calm himself. He spoke again, careful with his words. "Greensboro is a tiny town. If we were to be discovered... Weekly Wake would be over forever. You must follow my rules to stay unnoticed."

"What's the big deal? No one got hurt or arrested this time." Riley giggled, reminiscing the previous funeral.

Before their dad rebutted, Aspen stepped in to calm the fire. "We're sorry, Dad. We were just so excited to be there. It won't happen again."

"It definitely won't happen again. This is your last funeral for a while. Both of you."

"What?" the girls exclaimed in unison.

"You girls won't be allowed to attend another funeral until you learn to behave."

"But it's our family tradition! You can't have a family tradition without the whole family."

"I can't risk you two exposing us to the town."

"But -"

"Riley, I'm warning you, do *not* ask again."

The car fell silent. Riley muffled complaints to herself while Aspen accepted the punishment without grumbling. Aspen's eyes met her father's in the rearview mirror. He quickly reverted them, irritated. He knew Aspen was innocent, but he couldn't single out just one child from the funerals. Aspen would have to take one for the team. Although Nick hated to punish them, he couldn't jeopardize the sanctity of their Weekly Wake.

Weeks and weeks went by, and Nick did not budge. He'd kept the girls from the services for more than four weeks. To keep them busy, Aspen and Riley were enrolled in tennis lessons. Their new weekend routine was a morning session of doubles and then studying until 3 p.m. Their strict schedule allowed for a few hours of free time at night, which Riley used for binging TV shows. Riley didn't seem irritated about their new life. She was hardly bothered at all.

Meanwhile, Aspen grew frustrated. Weekly Wake was a Grays tradition that made her feel connected to the family, specifically, her late great grandmother, Amelia

Gray. Over the years, her dad would drop little hints, but he never shared his grandmother's full story. All she knew was that Amelia Gray was a beautiful woman with dark curls and deep maple eyes like hers. At twenty-one years old, Amelia fell in love with Ted, a high-profile stockbroker. Ted was clever, charming, successful—and married. But he promised his marital status would never stop him from loving her. After many years of painful separation, Ted had planned to run away with Amelia and leave his wife. Unfortunately, Ted was found dead the very next evening. The police report claimed suicide, but the truth was never uncovered.

Amelia had been distraught and devastated. She had had one goal when attending Ted's funeral: to finally declare her true feelings in front of everyone. The people deserved to know the heart of the person they were mourning. Amelia stood among the crowd and exposed Ted's love affair. Offended and disturbed by her oration, the group brutally scorned her. Amelia begged for someone to believe her, but she was shunned. To uphold her son's reputation, Ted's mother spread a false rumor that Amelia attended multiple funerals claiming to be the mystery mistress of successful men. Amelia was christened a liar. With malice in her heart, she embraced the lies told and acquired an insatiable hunger for revenge. Her bitterness grew and festered into a deep hatred for people. Unable to escape the lies of the town, she authored lies of her own. She scoured the neighboring cities with no remorse, planting lies and deceit at any funeral she could find.

She swore that if her name was to be slandered, she would manage her own remembrance and haunt the hearts of her adversaries. When Amelia had children of her own, she bred them to partake in her unusually disturbing practices. This caused her lineage to inherit intense pain and severe apathy towards death.

From that point on, the Gray family attended a new funeral every week to spread lies and make a mockery of death. This tradition lived on for generations and was eventually named the Weekly Wake. Aspen was especially fond of this occasion because it brought the family closer together. The funerals made her feel a part of something bigger than herself. Without this day, she felt incomplete.

With her funeral privileges revoked, her new weekend routine was void of excitement. Their parents would drop her and Riley off at tennis, then happily head to a new service. More than feeling down about the Weekly Wake, she missed her father. She missed dressing up and having somewhere special to go. Her black babydoll dress collected dust in the closet. And Riley was to blame.

One Saturday evening, their parents said their goodbyes and set off to another funeral. Aspen waited by the door with her parents. Riley sat comfortably, fixated on the living room TV screen.

"Aspen, make sure Riley stays out of trouble."

"Of course, Dad," she responded coldly. They turned to exit, and Aspen caught his coat. "Wait, Dad?"

"This again? The answer is no, Aspen," he spat angrily. For weeks, Aspen had begged her father to reconsider letting her rejoin the Weekly Wake. It had been so long since they'd gone as a family, and her weekends were becoming insufferable. His words were lined with frustration and slight disappointment. Aspen's eyes grew glossy, and she and her father held a glare, neither one wavering.

"I promise I'll be good. I'll sit in the ba-"

"Stop," her father commanded. He gripped her elbow and pulled her close. "Riley isn't ready. She's got a bit more growing up to do."

She tried once more. "Then, just let me come!"

"No one should have to grow up alone. Be a good sister."

Riley emerged from the living room after hearing them leave. "Is everything okay? What happened?"

"What do you mean 'what happened?' You're what happened! You ruined everything."

"You're still upset about the funerals? It's not that big of a deal."

"If it matters to me, it is a big deal. You don't decide things for me. I miss the funerals, I miss the family, you don't get it, Riley. I don't have people blowing up my phone or asking to hang out. The girls at school don't like me. And I don't like them. I spend my afternoons alone. I spend my weekends alone. All I have is this family. And now I'm basically kicked out."

"Okay, I get it."

"No, you don't get it. Dad was my favorite person. He was the only one who understood me, who made me feel safe. And now he hates me. You made him hate me, Riley."

Aspen began to cry.

"He doesn't hate you. Look, I didn't mean-"

"It doesn't matter what you meant to do, Riley. Weekly Wake is over. I don't need you to ruin anything else. Just leave me alone."

Aspen retreated upstairs to her bedroom. The two girls didn't see each other for the rest of the evening.

Later that night, Riley struggled to fall asleep. She replayed her sister's words a thousand times. Aspen was miserable, while Riley hadn't missed Weekly Wake at all. She considered it a relief not having to go. She wasn't afraid of ruining it because it didn't mean anything. But for Aspen, it mean everything. It seemed as though their family was falling apart and that Riley was to blame. Her heart grew heavy with anxiety. She stayed up all night contemplating how she would fix things for her sister. How she would make it up to Aspen and reunite their family. The night lasted a lifetime. By the end of her tossing and turning, she had developed a plan that would bring the family together and restore their cherished Weekly Wake. The solution was obvious to her.As the morning arrived, Aspen lightly shook Riley out of her sleep. "Hey, it's time to head to practice." She quickly left the room to avoid any further interaction.

Riley cleaned up, and soon the two girls were out the door.

Aspen unhooked her red bike from the wall and set it against their outside freezer. She stealthily surveyed Riley as she snapped her helmet on. The harsh silence and frowns created a less than joyful atmosphere. Aspen knew that her words from the night before had struck a chord with her sister. The remorse on her face was unconcealed. Although they weren't talking, Aspen's anger had subsided. However, she would not let Riley off the hook so quickly. If they were still banned from the Weekly Wake, why should she be forgiven so soon?

The girls began pedaling towards the main street. The streets were always busy in the morning. Aspen suggested the old creek trail to avoid heavy traffic, but Riley peddled to the streets anyway.

Aspen rode calmly and stayed close to the sidewalk. Once they were less than three miles from the court, Riley pedaled faster and faster, speeding across the asphalt. Aspen picked up her pace to catch-up. They rode side-by-side, neither speaking a word. Riley's mind raced with troubling thoughts. Ever so often, she'd steal a glance at her sister, hoping to see an ounce of forgiveness or a glimmer of softness. Aspen's face was stern. As they made it closer to the courts, Riley sped up even faster.

"Riley! Wait up!" Aspen shouted as her sister turned the corner. Aspen pedaled faster.

As their bike's realigned, Riley broke the silence. "I just want to say, I'm sorry," she said in an unsettling voice.

"Even if that was enough, it wouldn't mean anything to me. Those weekends meant everything, and you ruined that for me."

"I know that. You're right. I'm horrible." Riley began to stutter while tears fell from her face. "But I—I'm going to fix everything."

Confused, Aspen looked over to Riley. Aspen's face softened as she realized her sister was crying. She was letting it all impact her instead of brushing it off like she used to. Riley never cried like this. Aspen felt it was time to let up.

"Riley, I know you didn't-"

"Stop. You don't have to say anything."

The two girls locked eyes going more intensely. Aspen searched her sister's eyes to try and understand what she meant. How would she fix everything? And why was she pedaling so fast? Riley seemed so far away from the moment. Aspen wanted to reach out and pull her out of her drowning thoughts. Before she could find the words to say, Riley spoke.

"I'll give you one more funeral."

Suddenly, while maintaining painful eye contact, Riley threw herself into oncoming traffic.

A terrible shriek blared across the sky. Aspen slammed her breaks and was met with a gruesome scene.

The speed of the 2012 sedan swept up Riley's body and thrashed it against the windshield. The impact cracked the glass, slicing through her cheek and neck, drawing a thick line of blood across her side. The car slowed enough to allow the lifeless figure to slide across the roof and fall onto the hot asphalt.

Aspen sat petrified on her bike, distraught at the sight. Everything stopped. Her mind was at a standstill.

When people die in movies, it's slowed down. The distressed damsel is flung dramatically over a windshield, then slides gently to the ground. But this wasn't cinematic at all. There was no slow-motion edit or theatrical crash sound effect. It was raw, quick, and grossly surreal. 10 seconds ago, that body had breath in its lungs. It wasn't a body; it was my sister. And now it's not.

Bystanders quickly rushed to the scene, frantically dialing on their cellphones. In minutes, an ambulance was on its way. Her thoughts were muted by the sirens of disaster.

It was a foggy Saturday morning, and Aspen slowly rolled out of bed disturbed and determined to make it through the day. She took a cold shower, then got dressed in a long black dress with matching ballet flats. She considered finding something nicer to wear but decided against it.

Why should I feel pretty on a day like this? Why should I feel anything at all?

Aspen headed for the stairs and caught sight of her father, dressed in a crisp black shirt and matching pants. She immediately felt safe.

She trod down the staircase and fell into her father's arms. He wrapped himself around her frame and held her close. So many things had changed within the past few weeks. Normalcy was a distant relative with whom she was so far removed. She needed something to hold onto, to stabilize her. In her father's embrace, she found a place where she could fall apart.

As she looked up, she couldn't help but notice the disoriented look on her father's face. She thought she'd find devastation or disappointment. Instead, he seemed…lost. She couldn't entirely read him. As the clock turned, the trio exchanged warm looks and readied themselves.

The Grays walked bravely into the service. Immediately, Aspen felt burdened under the pitiful stares of the guests.

She re-gripped Nick's arm, clinging for strength. The attendees kept silent, with only a few mutters and whispers floating around the room. Aspen could hear the awful sentimental whispers, and it was draining.

"We are gathered here today…."

Everything around Aspen became muted. The whole service was somewhat melancholy. She felt like everyone was in on a big secret that excluded her. They were walking on eggshells, tiptoeing around a giant elephant.

During the wake, Aspen circled the room to greet and thank each guest individually. She couldn't help but notice how much easier it was to maneuver around a funeral you were supposed to be at. Quickly, Aspen's Aunt Cassie stole her attention.

"I know this can't be easy for you. I heard you and Riley were very close."

Aspen responded with no hesitation, "If by 'close' you mean 'strangling each other every day,' then yes, we were pretty much Thelma and Louis. Well, if Louis was killed by a 2012 Prius."

Aspen gave a light smile. Her aunt was greatly disturbed and slowly trailed off. Suddenly, Aspen felt reacquainted with herself.

Throughout the evening, she had more interactions similar to this. Something shifted once more people flooded the space. She was back in her element. Even after being banned for so long, her thrill for service-hopping never faltered. It wasn't the black dresses or any fascination with churches but there was something about death that made her feel alive. People came to funerals with a uniform sadness. Aspen craved the disturbing reaction on their faces when she did or said something out of 'funeral conduct.' And spreading lies! She could author the story of others, adding whatever details she desired, because the truth was buried. Lies could be true as long as the truth lied 6 feet under. Riley's funeral put Aspen on a high she'd never felt. Because of her relationship with the deceased, she was earning bigger reactions than ever before. It wasn't every day you had the chance to lie on your sister's grave. She fantasized how future funerals would go. Without Riley screwing things up and going too far, she could converse with people and disrupt things her way. And deceive with a grace Riley could only dream of. Her stories flowed free and uncensored.

With Riley gone, the repast felt…relaxed. *The reactions are funnier. The lies are wittier. I'm happier.*

As she looked across the room, she could see her father and mother smiling.

In an instant, Aspen ran over and squeezed in between the two. She sighed deeply.

"Everything will be okay, honeybee."

Nick softly squeezed his daughter's hand.

As the evening came to a close, the family of three stood against the church doors and expressed their gratitude.

"Remember. If you need anything, just call."

"Of course, I appreciate you. Thank you for coming," said Nick after giving his farewell to the last funeral attendee.

As the Gray family headed home, Aspen stretched out her arms and legs and relaxed into the cushioned back seat. A subtle grin grew on her lips. She had never been able to stretch out in the back seat before. There was so much more room. And she liked it. Her dad watched the road with one hand on the steering wheel and the other tucked underneath her mom's hand. He looked so serene. Aspen wrestled with conflicting feelings. How could she both love her sister *and* be satisfied with her absence? She prepared herself for impact, but the pain never hit. The grief was underwhelming. She asked herself, *If everyone is settled, is it such a bad thing to feel relieved?*

Her mom turned her shoulder and sweetly asked Aspen, "How are you feeling, sweetheart?"

Aspen breathed deep before answering honestly, "Better now."

Both parents turned to offer her a loving smile. As the family moved through the seemingly empty highway, Aspen turned her head to observe the frosted trees flying past. Tiny droplets attached themselves to her window as the rain began to fall. She took a breath of ease and found a calm stillness. Aspen's eyes lifted to the sky and she whispered, "Thank you, Riley."

FLIGHT ATTENDANT

"Thank you for choosing Delta Airlines. Welcome to Sacramento. It is partly cloudy with a high of sixty-three and a low of forty-eight. You may now unclip your seat belts. Please check your surroundings to make sure you haven't left anything. Be careful when collecting your bags from the overhead compartment. Whether you call Sacramento home or are just visiting, have a wonderful day. And once again, thank you for flying Delta Airlines."

I've been working as a flight attendant for ten years. And I've learned no attitude can't be corrected with a snarky but professional response. There's no nice way to put people in their place. Only a way that keeps your job and one that doesn't. The flight to Sacramento was a piece of cake. My hope is that flying back to L.A. will be just as easy. It's a short flight, but an hour and a half is plenty of time for people to act up. My goals for this flight are simple: get everyone boarded, filled with pretzels and soda, then put to sleep.

As the passengers begin to board the plane, I notice a woman lugging what seems to be her entire wardrobe behind her. I offer her a hand.

"Here, let me."

She pulls on my arm.

"Excuse me. I didn't give you permission to touch my things."

I put her bags back on the floor and give her an apologetic smile.

"My apologies."

So, she's that kind of passenger. Got it. I make a mental note to stay as far away from her as possible.

Once we are ready for take-off, I make my rounds, tightening seat belts and making movie recommendations for the duration of the trip. While I'm knee-deep in a captivating plot summary of *Ratatouille*, a familiar voice interrupts me. I turn around to see the same woman from earlier gesturing toward the overhead compartment with a pointed look.

"Can I get my makeup bag out? It will only take a second."

"I'm sorry, we're about to take off. It's not safe to re-open the overhead compartments."

I smile politely. This woman has been difficult since we've boarded. She's the typical overpacked and overly entitled passenger that seems to think I woke up this morning with the sole desire to please her.

"Sir, my lips are a desert, I just need my moisturizer."

"And I just need obedient passengers to sit quietly while the plane is departing. Thank you for your cooperation."

Every day, I'm surrounded by coughing, crying, and incessant fussing. If it's not one thing, it's another. At times, it's hard to tell if I'm a flight attendant or a babysitter. Then I remind myself that babysitters get paid more. In other news, my baby girl's twelfth birthday is tomorrow. For the last three weeks, she's been dropping me subtle hints of what she wants: a Kate Spade rose gold bangle. I told her if she scored the most points at her basketball game, I'd get her the exact one. To my dismay, she did. And now she expects jewelry. There are printouts on the fridge, sticky notes on all the doorknobs, and just yesterday, I found a papier-mâché replica of the bracelet on my car dashboard.

I'd planned on ordering the bracelet online, but just like my car insurance bill, I kept pushing it off. I may be able to stop by the mall before it closes. The sooner this flight is over, the better. After Moisturizer Lady, I don't have the patience for any more hassle. If I can make it home without any bumps, I'll be able to make it to the Kate Spade outlet before closing.

After the flight takes off, I tuck myself behind the cockpit and sink comfortably into my jump seat. A little boy around eight years old comes squirming down the center aisle clutching himself for dear life. Unfortunately for him, the bathroom is occupied.

"Hey, I'm sorry, but the bathroom is occupied. You need to return to your seat and wait there."

"But I really have to go!"

"I believe you. I really do. But someone's in there. So, as soon as that light turns green, you can go in."

"Fine."

"Alright."

I fist-bump the kid and send him back squirming down the center aisle. We're only twenty minutes in, and he already has to pee. Maybe the sodas and pretzels weren't such a good idea.

I glance up at the bathroom light every once in a while to check if it's green. It's funny, I don't remember seeing anyone go inside. Another fifteen minutes go by, and the light is still red. I start to feel sorry for the kid. I pack my cart with some snacks and make my rounds again.

"Hello, any snacks for you?

"Hi, any snacks for you all?"

"Hey there, any snacks for you all?"

As I inch towards the back, I notice Moisturizer Lady's seat is empty.

I bet she's hogging the bathroom.

The idea crawls under my skin and bites hard. I pass by the little boy and offer him and his parents a snack.

"Hi, any snacks for you all?"

He's still grabbing himself with eyes shut tight and knees buckled.

"Sir, has the light turned green yet?"

I glance back to check.

"No, it hasn't. Sorry, bud."

A middle-aged man who seems to be the kid's father speaks up. "Well, whoever is in the bathroom has been in there for like an hour."

Considering the duration of the flight is only an hour and a half, I know for sure it's been less than thirty minutes. But I understand how this works. I don't get paid to be right, I get paid to be polite.

"I will check on the passenger immediately. Thank you for your patience."

"Yeah, sure you will."

I turn my back and roll my eyes at the unnecessary rudeness. Either this man has trust issues, or he can tell when I'm lying. Reminds me a lot of my wife.

I drop off the snacks with the others, then make my way to the lavatory door. I knock three times.

No answer.

If she doesn't answer the second time, I'm gonna force open the door. I will brace myself for whatever horror waits on the other side. I knock again.

"Hi, is everything all right in there, ma'am?"

No answer.

I hate to do this, but Moisturizer Lady is pushing my buttons. I swear, if she's in there caking on makeup, I am going to be livid. I grab the master key and jimmy it through the keyhole. I open the door and see a man bent over splashing cold water on his face. It's not the Moisturizer Lady, it's Freddie from business class. He's the only flight attendant that frequents the bathroom more than any passenger. Flying makes him puke. The irony is uncanny. This job makes him sick.

Freddie looks up from the sink with a disturbed face.

"Is there a problem?"

Mmm, several. But any I care to address?

"No."

I quickly shut the door.

The plus side of my wonderful job is that I've built a strong immunity to germs. Unlike Freddie, I rarely ever get sick. Unfortunately, no amount of flights can help you build an immunity to people; I am still very allergic.

If that lady isn't in the bathroom or her seat, then where is she?

Once Freddie exits the lavatory, the sign flips to green, and I see the little boy spring from his seat and rush towards the door. I scoot past him and quickly scan each aisle. She's nowhere to be found. If I lose another passenger on a flight, there'll be hell to pay. And I don't like to pay for things unless I have a coupon.

I don't have a coupon.

I need to find her. I can't have this woman class-hopping. Not on my flight. I shut the curtain separating coach from business class and begin the search. She can't have gone far.

As I enter business class, I'm greeted with a comfortable silence. It's so peaceful in business class. Everyone is either on their laptop or fast asleep. No one is drinking, eating, or aggravating the attendants. It's heaven on earth. There's no sign of Moisturizer Lady here. Maybe she left her seat and is in another bathroom. If that's it, then I look like a creep following her around. I find a trash bag and pretend to pick up soda cans along the aisle. While I'm waiting for the person to come out of the bathroom, I notice someone trying to get my attention.

"Excuse me, could I have more wine?" a young woman on her laptop asks, interrupting my search.

"Sorry, I don't work here."

My eyes continue to scan the rows for her.

The lavatory light flips to green, and a man waddles out of the bathroom. I release a sigh and throw the trash bag in a corner. Onto first class.

As I walk through the curtain separating business and first-class, my virgin eyes are quickly met with Delta's most prized uncooperative passenger.

I don't know exactly what I'm looking at.

Moisturizer Lady is sprawled out in the center aisle with two hands on the ground and her behind in the air. She's doing yoga. In the middle of a plane ride. This is unbelievable. As she twists and bends her body into different positions, I see other passengers step over her. How long has she been doing this? And where is the first-class attendant?

I stretch my neck towards the front of the cabin and see Leonard snoozing it up in his jump seat. Ladies and gentlemen, your Delta flight attendants. I'll have to take care of this myself.

"Ma'am, what do you think you're doing?"

"It's called Hatha Yoga, it enhances your mind, strength, and balance."

"Umm…cool. I love a good yoga session, but why are you doing it here?"

"Coach was too small. I needed a bigger aisle."

"Well, unfortunately, you are not allowed in first class, and under no circumstances are you allowed to do aerobic exercises on a plane."

"Fine, just let me finish this pose."

"Ma'am, I need you to return to your seat."

Just then, a woman around her age approaches. "Excuse me."

Not knowing if she's talking to me or Moisturizer Lady, we both turn and look.

"May I join you?" She's a tiny lady who looks to be in her late forties.

"Of course, I have a spare mat in my bag." Moisturizer Lady shoots me a smile. "Fetch it for me? You know where I sit."

Is she serious?

"I won't be fetching anything. You won't be joining her, and you will both be going back to your seat."

"Why are you disturbing my zen?"

"Because you're disturbing my passengers!"

"No, sir, I'm building community."

At this point, my blood pressure is as high as the plane's altitude. It's only been an hour, and I have nothing under control. I must get these women back in their seats before landing. If anything happens to them during this flight, I will be held responsible. I won't be driving to the outlets after work but to corporate to hand in my badge and vest.

"You could use more zen in your life; it might inspire you to want more for your career."

"First of all, flight attending is a very respectable career. Secondly, you need to go back to your seat."

I'm trying my best to deflate the situation, but I don't know what else I can do. I softly tug at Moisturizer Lady's mat, willing her to move.

"Hey! You don't have permission to touch my mat!" she yells, drawing the attention of others.

Leonard jolts awake.

I try to lift her mat again, but she swats my hand away. I'm running out of appropriate responses. Management usually frowns upon fighting or assaulting the passengers, so I need to handle this issue with grace. I just need to decide if that grace will include using my taser.

"Miss, I'm going to help you up so that you can return to...."

As I reach for her wrist, she turns over her shoulder and kicks me in the chest. I stumble back and gasp for air.

She just hit me. I think I'm ready to lose my job.

The other passengers rise to see the commotion. Moisturizer Lady leaps from the ground and flings herself towards me. She is out of control. I catch her body in my arms. She twists and turns herself, squirming every which way. I restrict her arms and try to quiet her as she screams down the aisle. I don't get paid enough for this. She whips her elbow back, jamming it into my jaw. I lose my grip and drop her on the floor, knocking my badge off. I really don't get paid enough for this.

After my one-on-one wrestling match, I see my two coworkers staring as if this is a ticketed event.

"Can I get some help?"

Leonard and Freddie finally make their way to us and detain the woman. Moisturizer Lady is kicking and screaming as they carry her back to coach.

I release a breath of relief and check my face for any blood. I press my fingers against the place it burns; minor nosebleed, mostly sweat. Moisturizer Lady is gone, and my heart is still beating out of my chest. I really need to work out more.

I bend down to feel for where my badge had dropped. It better not be bent or scratched. The other passengers ask me if I need help. Forgetting I'm at work, I answer, "Back off!"

I'm surrounded by blank stares.

"Sorry," I mutter, embarrassed about my outburst.

This altercation has quickly placed me in a mood.

As I regroup and pick up the bloodstained yoga mat, I notice a small glistening band underneath the seat. I crouch down to get a better look, and there it is! It's the Kate Spade rose gold bangle. I rub my eyes to make sure I'm not hallucinating. I grab the bracelet and inspect it closely. Gold trim, check; New York engravement, check; width two point two seven inches, probably not, but we can get it altered. It's almost perfect! Except for the fact that it belongs to someone else. Probably someone in this aisle. I rise from the floor and address the passengers beside me.

"Excuse me, does this belong to you?" I ask a woman.

"Nah, I'm pretty sure it flew off that lady's hand when she was carried off."

"Thanks."

"No prob!"

Hmm. So, this bracelet belongs to Moisturizer Lady. Very interesting.

Please make sure your seatbelts are fastened and all large electronics are put away. We are preparing for landing. It should be about ten minutes. Welcome to Los Angeles.

I make my way back to my seat and stare lovingly at the piece of jewelry on my lap. Is God finally rewarding me for keeping the peace and spreading joy to passengers? Could this be the rose gold lining that makes this horrid flight worth it? Everything seems to be falling into place. The flight is almost over, Moisturizer Lady is in custody, and the Kate Spade bangle is in my hand. I didn't write this ending; it's fate! The airline gods have clearly put this bracelet in my path for a reason, so who am I to deny it? It's truly a picture-perfect ending.

Unfortunately, my conscience imposes itself on the situation. I can't ignore the obvious moral compromise. I never consider myself to be a saint, but stealing? What type of person would that make me? Could I really live with myself if I gifted my daughter a stolen bracelet?

Yes, I could.

We have a soft landing and begin to prepare the airstairs for the passengers. We disembark the rest of the plane in record time. People are in a rush to leave since the whole yoga debacle. Who would've thought that a flight could be so dramatic? It was an eventful flight, to say the least. I may have gotten the lights knocked out of me, but now I have a birthday gift for my daughter. I have no regrets.

We begin the sweep-through of our respective cabins, picking up any trash or forgotten belongings. As I reach for a package of hummus someone was nice enough to leave behind, I try to forget the fact that there's a stolen bracelet burning a hole in my pocket. After finishing up, the crew meets at the front of the plane.

"Before you all head out, the yoga lady said she's missing a bracelet. Did you guys see anything?" Freddie asks us.

My heart skips a beat, and I swallow deeply. The other guys shake their heads absentmindedly. I clear my throat and say with confidence, "No."

I grab my things and head towards the exit. My phone buzzes, and it's a text from my daughter. "Hi, Dad! Will you be home soon?"

I glance up from my phone and see Freddie and Leonard approaching. Leonard pats me on the back.

"That was ridiculous, man, I can't believe you got kicked in the face."

"Yeah, I wish we were there to help before you got beat down," Freddie adds.

"I wouldn't necessarily call it a beat down, but yes, this was an eventful flight."

I look back to my phone and gratefully respond: "I'll be home soon, sweetie. And I have a surprise for you."

As I slide my phone back into my pocket, the three of us make our way through the crowds. I see Moisturizer Lady getting escorted into the back of some cop's sedan. Our eyes lock. She looks the same as she did on the plane. Her hair tousled and veins bursting violently from her arms.

She looks like she wants to kill me. As we walk past her, I clasp my hands together and gift her a sarcastic smile. I must acknowledge this woman's tenacity. Her stubbornness and disobedience never wavered, no matter how many warnings I gave her. I've never encountered a passenger who was so passionately defiant. It was impressive. Moisturizer Lady will be detained but never forgotten.

"Why does this stuff always happen on our flights. I bet this never happens at JetBlue," Freddie complains

"It seems like you always get the worst sections. I'd be stressed out if that happened to me. You gonna try and get some free vacation from this?"

"Haha, not at all. I'm fine. And besides, I realized something after my years of working here." I feel for the outline of my daughter's bangle pressed deep within my pocket. "Everything happens for a reason."

SOCCER MOMS

Lisa pulls into the parking lot, confident she'll claim her rightful spot as head of snacks, impress all the parents, and win the admiration of all the players. Lisa sports a 2018 Kia Sorento with a license plate that reads, "Go Team!" She is unmistakably a die-hard soccer mom. And the best, if you ask her.

The field is packed with six-to-seven-year-old children in soccer jerseys packing up to go home. Parents casually threaten their kids to grab their water bottles, shin guards, and other soccer paraphernalia.

"Mom, I really have to go!" yells Lisa's son from the back seat. Timmy is a six-year-old obsessed with Godzilla and only moderately amused by soccer. Some players bring excitement, speed, and athleticism to the game; Timmy brings his Hydro Flask. With his knees glued together, he squirms incessantly. "Come on, Mom, I need to pee!"

"Honey, our spot is right next to the porta-potty. Okay? Just wait a few more minutes, then you can go."

The parking lot is backed up. She waits, slightly irritated, humming to herself, *this is why we leave the house*

BULLDOG

early, Lisa. The first three cars respectively skip over her spot. But to her surprise, the fourth car swings in without a care in the world.

She chuckles incredulously.

"Looks like we've got a newbie. Someone's in Mommy's spot."

She temporarily pulls into the spot right next to it. As she comes tire to tire with the uninformed driver, she rolls down her window.

Amy, in her late twenties, is driving a more modern 2021 Audi 5 Sportback. She's younger, peppier, friendlier, and an overall better person. She springs out of her nice car and waves her son off as he meets up with the other players. Lisa gets out of the car to meet her.

She greets Amy with a suspicious charm. "Hi! I don't think we've met. I'm Lisa."

Amy matches her energy. "Amy. Nice to meet you."

"Hey, before you get settled, small thing, I usually park in that spot."

"Oh! I'm so sorry!"

"It's so small, really!"

"I had no idea!"

"It's so minuscule. So, so tiny."

"Well, I guess next time I'll know," Amy casually remarks. She pops the trunk and starts to unload. Lisa watches her movements. Meanwhile, she's forgotten to let her son out of the car. Rocking and crossing his legs, he tries not to wet himself.

"Totally, don't worry about it now. It can wait until after you unload everything. In fact -"

She calls out for Timmy to come out and help with supplies.

"Oh, don't worry about it. I've got it."

She nods and goes to get her own stuff. Lisa pops her trunk and pulls out her very impressive Red twenty-four-quart igloo cooler.

At least, she thinks it's impressive until Amy pulls out her superior forty-five-quart Canyon Hard Cooler and a gorgeous luxury soft cooler.

"Wow, all that for your son? You really come prepared! I love to see it."

"Well, not just for my son. For the whole team."

Lisa's body and pride are stricken with disgust. An extreme but one-sided tension surrounds the two moms. Without batting an eye, Amy continues to unload her car, unaware of Lisa's brewing anger. Still stranded in the back seat of the vehicle, Timmy yells in desperation, "Mom! The door is locked. I need to go to the bathroom."

"Excuse me, Timmy," Lisa says in an astonished tone. "Do not interrupt Mommy when she is having an altercation. That's very rude."

She quickly reverts her energy to her prevailing rival. "That's very generous, but I do the snacks for the kids."

"Oh, nice!"

"Yeah, I make homemade energy bars. The kids love 'em."

"Homemade, huh?"

Lisa picks up on her condescending tone. She sidesteps the implication with a smile.

"Brenda's kid has a peanut, gluten, and wheat allergy, so it's easier just to make stuff at home that everyone can eat."

"Well, that's very considerate of you."

"I enjoy it. I really do."

Amy continues to unload her snacks. She has Oreos, Capri Sun juices, cheese sticks, Gatorade, and other pre-packaged snacks.

"Well, now the kids can have a variety!"

Lisa's face twitches a little bit.

"What do you mean?"

"Well, the kids might want to mix things up a little."

"They don't need to mix things up."

"You know, add some spice to their weekend."

"They don't like spice; they like my energy bars."

They share a polite smile.

Amy attempts to de-escalate the issue. "It's really not a big deal. You don't have to get upset."

Lisa bends over, reaching for her pack of extra water. "I'm not getting upset; I'm getting water."

"Okay, I get it. I'm not trying to ruffle any feathers."

"No no no. Ruffle away! I'm super flexible. My motto has always been: *a helpful parent is a loving parent.* So, if you wanna help, I'm grateful."

"Awesome. I really would just like to help out."

Amy flashes Lisa a genuine smile. Lisa rummages through her trunk to retrieve her ruby-red lawn chair; she responds without even glancing in Amy's direction.

"And we love to have you—; I just find it interesting that you believe ruining our kids' health is *helpful.*"

Amy's smile drops. "What are you talking about?"

"I just think you should be careful about pushing your snack propaganda into the minds of these kids."

Lisa and Amy stand face to face, each holding their coolers in hand. Amy's calm look falters as offense contorts her face. She quickly defends her honor. "Hmmm, well, pre-packaged snacks are more covid-friendly."

"How is a snack more friendly? Does it pick up the tab after dinner or offer to drive you to the airport? I'm just curious. I didn't know snacks could be so considerate."

"Name-brand snacks make the parents feel more comfortable."

"Interesting. Processed fats and added sugars don't usually bring people comfort. Just diabetes."

Amy rolls her eyes. "Look, I was just trying to—"

"Diabetes, Amy."

"Okay—"

"I'm just looking out for them, Amy."

Amy is exhausted by Lisa's dramatics. Lisa suppresses—or, rather, conceals—her irritation. She shifts the conversation.

"How long have you been with the Bulldogs?"

"Since Timmy was three years old. But we missed last season."

"What happened last season?"

"Timmy needed a break to rest."

"Not enough energy from those bars, huh?"

Lisa deadpans, visibly offended, "He was sick."

"Hmm. Well, during your son's little sabbatical, the league edited quite a few of its bylaws."

"What are you talking about?" She's unconvinced.

"The health standards, procedures, everything. But you have so much stuff, I'm sure you're prepared."

Lisa swallows nervously, afraid of what she's about to hear.

"You made sure Timmy was covid tested at least a week prior, right? And packed two extra masks? One for the second half and one for the post-game?"

"Of course."

She's bluffing.

"And you packed disinfecting wipes to wipe down your chairs? And brought lotion to help with the dryness from hand sanitizer?"

A complex and determining moment passes between them. Both ladies are frustrated and deeply impressed with the other. Never had either of them met mothers with such commitment to the health and well-being of a recreational soccer team.

Lisa, particularly astonished by Amy's persistence, decides

it's time to end things. It's time for the ultimate showdown.

"I know what you're trying to do, but it's not going to work. The unofficial title of comfort coordinator has been and always will be mine. And I'll be dam-"

As her tone gets increasingly aggressive, she achieves the attention of concerned parents.

"I'll be disgruntled," she corrects herself, her voice falling to a menacing whisper, "if I let some off-brand barbie swoop in and steal the show. I didn't want to do this, but you've left me no choice."

Lisa grabs her extra-large duffle bag with *Best Soccer Mom* embedded with red and blue thread.

Lisa walks proudly to the center of the street and extends her arm. While sustaining a hard stare, she drops the bag on the ground at Amy's feet. Amy follows her lead and places her bag on the ground. Both ladies kneel on the asphalt, ready to share what they've brought.

And the war begins.

"Extra socks?" Lisa challenges.

Amy accepts the challenge. "Check."

"Extra shin guards?" Lisa smirks.

"Check." Amy holds up the item with a prideful grin.

Amy then takes the reins and begins to challenge Lisa. "Cooling towel?"

"Check," Lisa reluctantly answers, uncomfortable with the power shift.

"Sunscreen?"

"Oh, please." Lisa rolls her eyes, pulling out an SPF 50 bottled lotion and one spray bottle.

Amy and Lisa stare hard before blasting into serious showdown mode. Both mothers begin rapidly pulling out items to one-up each other. They flash their items so quickly neither of them is keeping up.

Amy and Lisa continue the battle; meanwhile, the referee and coach are chatting with each other. Each of them is growing increasingly upset. The referee eventually throws his hands up in surrender. The coach jogs over to Amy and Lisa.

"The other team showed up with the wrong-colored jerseys, so the Bulldogs are in blue today. You brought your sons' blue jersey, right?"

With wide eyes, both Lisa and Amy's faces fall bleak.

Lisa quickly retorts, "Yes, of course, I did. I could never forget something so fundamental."

Amy also has a quick response: "Definitely, I have his blue uniform in the backseat. No problem at all."

As the coach leaves their presence, a silence falls between the two. Both wear a visibly panicked look that they are working all too hard to hide. They frantically search their bags for a jersey that will prove their superiority. Amy quits the search after a few minutes, while Lisa continues a bit longer, desperate to come out on top. After a while, neither of them finds their sons' jersey.

Lisa puts the blame on her husband. "You know what,

it must have slipped out of my bag this morning when my husband loaded the trunk."

Amy takes the blame. "Well, I just forgot it."

Lisa is distraught by her honesty.

"I guess we're not perfect, huh?"

"I mean, I technically didn't forget mine, it just fell out. Because of my husband."

Amy chuckles at Lisa's stubbornness.

"Lisa, we forgot. Just accept it."

Lisa closes her eyes and takes a deep breath. For the first time in all her years of *Soccer Mom-ing*, she forgot the alternate jersey. Who knew a polyester cloth would be the fall of her legacy. Maybe there was room for two snack moms on the team after all. She asks herself if she could share the glory with another mom. *Yes, I could,* she answers.

Lisa swallows her pride, relaxing her tense muscles.

"Amy, you're an amazing soccer mom. I'm sorry for making you prove yourself."

Amy attempts to make amends. "And I'm sorry for trying to one-up you. We don't have it all together, but we're trying our best and that's what matters."

Lisa smiles genuinely. "I couldn't agree more."

The two ladies begin to pack up and head back to their cars.

"I'm about fifteen minutes out, so I should be back after warm-ups," Lisa says.

"Ugh, I'm thirty minutes out. Stevie might miss the

first half," Amy complains, leaning her elbow against the open driver's door.

"Oh no, I'm sorry," Lisa sympathizes. She sincerely feels bad for Amy. As much as it pains her to discover she has forgotten the jersey, she has to admit, it's a nice feeling to be just as unprepared as someone else. They were screw-ups together.

"Yeah, I'll just try to-"

Amy stops abruptly. With her bag draped over her shoulder, she does a double-take. Tucked under a pair of socks, she spots a bright blue cloth. She pulls on the fabric, and there it is: her son's alternate jersey. She holds it up for Lisa to see and smiles.

"Well, look at that." Amy perks up.

Lisa's smile falls to a frown. Her blood boils. Every nice thing she thought about Amy goes out the window. She hates her.

"Mom?" Timmy calls nervously.

She finally turns her full attention to him in the peak of frustration. "*Yes*, Timmy!"

She opens the back door and sees *her* son's jersey! It's peeking out from under Timmy. He's been sitting on it this whole time. She quickly grabs it and looks for Amy. She proudly holds it up.

"Well, look at that!" She proclaims obnoxiously.

She feels droplets running down her arm. The jersey is soaked in urine. Timmy climbs out of the car with his head hung low. Amy offers a sympathetic smile.

"Sorry, Mom. But don't worry, we never wear the blue jerseys anyway."

Without a word, Lisa packs the wet jersey into her duffle bag and hops into the driver's seat. She puts the key in the ignition and starts the car.

"Go warm up with the team. Tell your coach I'll be back by halftime."

Timmy nods and sprints towards the team. As he's halfway to the field, he turns around and asks, "Am I in trouble?"

"No, babe, you're fine. Have fun!"

Lisa watches as her son joins the other players. With a mismatched jersey and damp shorts, Timmy nonetheless leaps onto the field, ready to support his team.

She rests her head on the steering wheel in distress. This is the fall of her reign. A moment she'll never forget. Beginning with a small parking lot debacle, she could have never imagined things would get this dark. She came in second place, and the consolation prize was an arm reeking of pee. She has been dethroned and forced to sit in filth. She is no longer the kingpin and feels she has lost all field-cred. *Soccer mom-ing* is her identity—who is she, if not the most reliable and awesome soccer mom? She lifts her gaze and is met with the other parents laughing and smiling. Her nose flares in disgust watching the parents continue in her absence. Darkness falls upon her eyes and determination fills her heart.

"I will not be made a fool," she mutters to herself. "I will restore what is right, I will make my energy bars, and I...will...be...avenged!"

NASHVILLE

Fagerland Family Assigned Roles:

Dad – Learning duty: News, politics, new language, reading, etc.

Mom – Cooking duty: Breakfast, lunch, dinner, snacks, cocktails, ice cream, etc.

River – Entertainment duty: Board games, movies, vacations, TV, etc.

Emil – Cleaning duty: Washing dishes, laundry, bedrooms, trash, etc.

Sierra – Physical Health duty: Workouts, sports, hikes, yoga, etc.

My name is Emil Fagerland and I am my mother's favorite middle child. As you can see from the list above, I am in charge of cleaning the household. I'm reasonably gifted at it. I'd say I'm a pristine, proficient, and proper sanitation specialist. I know my way around a vacuum and could recite the top five cleaning solutions off the top of my clean-shaven head. I've honed this skill for as long as I can remember and maintain this custodian position with great ease. The only matter that infests my mind is the unfortunate fact that I absolutely, positively, and without doubt despise cleaning.

Since I was a young child, I've been the sanitation specialist in my family. It was essentially my birthright. For the last three generations, the Fagerlands have experimented with what Great-Grandpa called "harmonious labor." Its purpose? To add fluidity, coherence, and balance to the family unit. The effect? To add misery to my daily life. With everyone's rules succinctly outlined, there's no room for confusion or individuality.

The practice was inspired by the *dao* from the *Analects of Confucius*. It takes a lot of elements from filial piety and applies some modern traits as well. Harmonious labor is not like a religion or a thing the family all has in common; it's our way of living. It's a lifestyle. And it's all I've ever known. For years, it's been adopted within the Chinese culture. We're not Chinese, so I never really understood why it's been a family practice for so long. But it's a part of us, and I fear it always will be. Fast forward three generations, it is now time to assume my responsibilities.

"One more round, Emil, come on!" my brother River cries. Mom, Dad, River, and Sierra are huddled on the couch, approaching hour four of our weekly game night. The best thing about my role is that it always resurfaces in situations you'd never imagine. I never run out of work, and I'm never off duty.

"If you're gonna help sanitize all the controllers, then we can play unlimited rounds." The room goes quiet at my mention of River helping me clean. Asking a family member to operate outside their commitment is like asking a chef to make you a PB & J sandwich. It is an abomination to Fagerlands everywhere. Not PB & Js, but doing other people's jobs. Even considering this increased my chances of starting a riot.

My dad quickly interjects to ease the tension: "Oh, Emil was just joking around. Nice, Emil, funny."

Leave it to my dad to pervert my pure complaint into a joke.

I ease up and put on a smile. We resume playing another forty-minute round of Super Smash Bros. It didn't matter that our bedtime was in sixty minutes and I'd be up late wiping down the game console; all that mattered was that the family enjoyed it. That's all that ever mattered.

"Goodnight, everyone," my siblings sing in unison. *They're precious.*

As my family slowly climbs the stairs to their respective sleeping quarters, I stay behind to mop and take care of the remains of my family's late-night snack. I see my father's plate on the table and grip it with more force than any dinnerware deserves. While scrubbing at the grease, I begin to think.

What am I doing here? I don't want to throw my life away doing chores. I'd rather throw it away…designing an app, or going to school for theatre. If I dedicate my time to sweeping and dusting, what will I have to show for it? I don't want to tell my grandchildren that I spent most of my young life cleaning out a refrigerator. How will this role affect me in the long run? These questions aren't coming out of nowhere. At age sixteen, I've found myself at a crossroads.

It's only a week until my final confirmation, where I'll swear the rest of my young life to this custodian position. If I confirm, I'll be cleaning for the family until the age of twenty-six. It's an outward declaration of an inward commitment. In our culture, only males have a confirmation day, leaving the females to work until their father sees fit for a change. Kinda messed up when you think about it, but they marry out of the family. And believe it or not, wives have easier jobs than daughters. So, it's a trade-off.

The confirmation festivities are like any other gathering: We fellowship, break bread, sell ourselves to the laborious work of the family, and then have cake. River's confirmation went just like that. He stood among our family and friends and accepted his role with no hesitation. Mom and Dad had been so proud of him. If my job was entertainment, I wouldn't hesitate to confirm either. But, with my position being a little less glamorous, you can understand my trepidation. Something tells me my ceremony will be a little different. It may result in a mess too big for even me to clean up.

But for now, all I have to decide is whether to use a bristle brush or a Brillo pad to scrape the dried sauce off my dad's plate. Since my dad insists on extra "everything," it always takes me an extra minute to clean his plate.

I don't like my father.

I go to bed around twenty-five minutes later than usual. I know it's wrong to do, but I march loudly upstairs towards my room in hopes of disturbing as many of them as possible. They need to hear my frustration, and they need to feel bad about it.

As I lie in bed, two difficult decisions weigh heavy on my heart: *will I say yes or no tomorrow?* and *what the heck would I do instead?* I close my eyes to escape the thoughts and pray that God will take a bottle of lemon-scented Windex and wipe away all my issues.

CONFIRMATION DAY

As my family and friends gather in our living quarters, I can feel the nerves roaming through my body. Today is supposed to be this grand celebration, but no one is going to celebrate what I have to say. I decided early this morning that I'm going to decline the position. I went back and forth all night. But, after my parents woke me up at 6 a.m. because their sheets were, "not as white as they could be," I made my choice. I'll have to thank them someday for making the decision clear.

I walk through the house with my best behavior intact. I smile and say hello to everyone that's arrived to support me. It's not easy walking around and giving fake smiles, but I honestly don't know what else to do. In a perfect world, I would sit down with my parents and have a heart-to-heart. Tell them about how I'm feeling and ask them for a different role in the family. Unfortunately, we Fagerlands are suckers for a good drama. So, I wait for the most significant moment on the biggest stage to speak my truth.

Minutes before my speech, I rush to clean up the excess mess in the kitchen. After tossing out a few cups and wiping down the countertop, I'm relaxed. I can't very well be seen tidying up after I formally quit. So, I have to get all this anxiety out now. As I hastily spray more solution onto the countertop, I see my father approaching from the corner of my eye. It's time.

With a microphone in one hand and a chilled cider in the other, my father takes the stage to introduce me to the party guests. "Thank you all for coming out to celebrate my son on his confirmation day. Emil is passionate, loyal, obedient, and by far the best dang sanitation specialist there is. But I know I'm a little biased."

The crowd releases a few chuckles. I inwardly roll my eyes and make my way to the podium. I give my father a corporate side hug and start my address.

"Today, I'm making a decision that will transform the next ten years of my life. I'm grateful for the opportunity to pledge my honor, respect, and service to my family as the sanitation specialist. As many of you know, I've been in this position for almost as long as I've been alive. I was trained in-house by my mother and have learned all there is to know about cleanliness and upkeep. It's been a pleasure sanitizing our sanctuary and helping my mother make this house a home. I truly believe everyone in my family was assigned the perfect role. My father is easily the smartest man you'll ever meet, a true educator. My mother is a wizard in the kitchen; I still salivate when I think of her homemade Oreo cheesecake. Sierra has been active since she was in diapers, and River is a gifted entertainer. He'll be on TV one day for sure. Everyone in my family is perfect for their role, except for me."

The audience gasps loudly. Some laugh awkwardly as if waiting for the "just kidding." But I can't be more serious. This is me finally shattering the family's illusion that I'm happy. I'm done playing the role of a good, obedient busboy.

I re-grip the mic, inhale deeply, and deliver what I have to say as clearly as possible.

"I can't believe I've lasted this long in such a miserable position. I'm honestly not sure why anyone would willingly dedicate their life to cleaning. It's embarrassing to know my parents sincerely thought I was happy this whole time. The idea that I'm supposed to yield to their every beck and call is absurd. And to be quite frank—I'm pissed."

The crowd gasps even louder. Their startled reaction gives me exactly what I need to continue on my soapbox. I grab a sip of water, loosen my tie, and begin my next set.

"I'm pretty sure cleaning is a poorer sentence than death. I physically can't even say the word *cleaning* without feeling a slight twitch in my left eye. Don't get me wrong, I respect those who clean for a living. Society needs individuals willing to serve and clean up after others. Unfortunately, I'm not one of those sad individuals. I need to take some time off to figure out what I want. I appreciate the memories I've accrued over the years and will always love my family. However, I must make myself clear to avoid any further confusion: I'd rather be beaten, tied up, and left in a ditch to die than clean another plate for this family."

The room falls completely silent.

"I humbly and respectfully denounce my position as sanitation specialist in the family. Thank you."

I set the microphone down and hop off the stage. As I'm reacquainted with my seat, I stare deliciously at the reactions written on my family's faces. My two siblings' jaws have dropped, my mother is in tears, and my father... Well, he visibly wants to hurt me.

After many painfully awkward conversations and apologies, the party comes to an end. I don't feel guilty and I'm not sorry, but a good Norwegian boy like myself hates to see his guests upset. So, when I serve the dessert, every slice of cake is paired with its own personal atonement.

My Aunt, Ingrid, is especially disappointed because we'd arranged for me to clean out her closet in two weeks. I may still drop by and help out. I'm fed up, not cruel.

"Thank you for coming; I hope you enjoyed the cake."

"Yes, I was serious."

"Yes, I hate cleaning. Have a good weekend!"

I shake hands and greet as many people as possible. I want them to know that while I appreciate them coming to support me, my decision is final. There would be no convincing or changing my mind.

As the guests leave, I clean up the garbage left in the backyard, then head inside. To be honest, I'm not sure what the next step is. I've only read a few testimonials on what happens when you deny your position. It usually results in a classic disowning situation or a mysterious disappearance. Neither of which I'm an advocate for.

It's been almost an hour since the party and my parents haven't said a word to me.

I consider approaching them to gauge their anger. But dinner comes sooner than I think.

Within the first twenty seconds of dinner, I get a clear picture of how angry my parents are. It's pretty easy to measure your dad's anger when he's "accidentally" kicking you underneath the table. He won't take his eyes off me. Sierra breaks the silence by raving about her new custom-made HIIT routine for us to try on Monday. I give her a quiet "thanks for the effort" smile. The table remains quiet.

I beg River to cancel our post-dinner game session for tonight, but he insists. He thinks it may ease the tension. I'm not sure how Mario Party can make my dad hate me less, but it's worth a try.

We all go to bed on time. I sleep with heavy thoughts. I figured my decision would make my life better in some ways, but it seems to have added more drama. While satisfied with my choice, I can't help but worry about the repercussions.

What will happen tomorrow? Where will I sleep tomorrow night? I try my best to subside these thoughts.

The following day, I wake up to a note on my bedside table.

Good morning, Emil. This morning, I took my wife and kids to breakfast. We'll be home around noon. We can talk when we get home.

I wish I could say this note is a surprise, but it's my father. He's notoriously dramatic and terribly emotional. I guess he's not calling me 'son' anymore. If I knew denying my position would make me lose out on pancakes, I wouldn't have... No, I still would've quit.

I roll slowly out of my sheets and go into the bathroom. When I flip on the lights, I find another note. I'll have to remind myself to throw out the sticky notes next time I upset my father.

The small note on the bathroom mirror read: *Because you've deprived me and the rest of our family of a clean home, here's a reminder of what filth looks like.*

I look down and see he's thrown a pile of rubber bands onto the floor, hairbrushes, and clippers. They are all scattered across the tiles. After lifting one of the brushes, I see that it's stuck to what seems to be toothpaste.

I do my best to ignore the obvious trap and brush my beautiful head of hair.

After a few runs with my brush, I hear the side door open. I walk across the hall and see my siblings stroll happily through the doors with leftover flapjacks in a Styrofoam container.

River asks me if I'm hungry. Dad intercepts the exchange and flings the flapjacks onto the floor.

"No pancakes for him; outsiders don't get pancakes."

I roll my eyes while River picks up the fallen cakes. My father shoots his eyes towards me.

"You're the outsider," he clarifies.

"Thank you for clarifying," I reply.

My parents sit me down in the living room and finally have the highly anticipated conversation. Nothing could have prepared me for what they'd say. Or, more accurately, what they wouldn't say.

My father gives me a hard stare for the first thirty seconds, which I interpret as the intimidation portion of our heart-to-heart. I try my best to look adequately intimidated. After his face persists, the feelings become real, and I start to prepare my heart to be reprimanded. I have to say, his stare is pretty effective.

"Your speech came as a shock to your mother and me."

I nod.

"After discussing it together, we've decided that we do not like it."

"Okay."

"And upon further deliberation, we have concluded that your presence in this household is no longer required. As of March fourth, you will be removed."

I've never heard such horrible words packaged so delicately. He said it so sweetly, I thought I misheard it.

"Removed?"

"Yes, Emil, did you really think we were gonna let you just prance around this house after what you said at the party? We may be your parents, but we have feelings."

This is not how I expected the conversation to go. Are they really this upset? I knew they would give me the cold shoulder, but all of this! What will happen now? Am I losing my family? Where will I go? Yea… I should probably ask that question.

"Where will I go?"

"Nashville. We booked you a one-way ticket."

"Why?"

"Because actions have consequences, Emil."

"But why Nashville?"

"Because Willy Nelson lives in Nashville."

"Who on earth is Willy Nelson?"

My mother lays a hand on father's shoulder and politely interjects.

"Willy is a musical legend, Emil, you know…'On the Road Again,' 'Crazy,' he's very famous."

"Look, boy, all you need to know is that I hate Willy Nelson. And by sending you to Nashville, I can make sure all my nuisances live in one place."

It doesn't take long for my father to work himself into a rage. I made the fatal mistake of asking why he hates Willy Nelson, and his tangent goes on for about an hour. Eventually, mother calms him down, and the attention reverts to me.

There isn't much left for me to say; my parents made up their minds. I'd refused to make my bed, and now I have to lie in it.

MARCH 4

It's the morning of March fourth, and my brother and sister pull me into a tight embrace.

"You guys will be okay; we'll still talk on the phone and play video games online."

They look considerably sad, and that makes me feel better. I then turn my attention to my mother. She's standing in the door frame with tears forming in her eyes. She's one hug away from breaking. I hold her close.

As we break, I feel something slide carefully into my pocket. She whispers, "For food and travel."

We have a mutual understanding that my father doesn't need to know about.

The last person to say goodbye to is my father. I pick up my suitcase and see him standing across the room. He has a broom in one hand and a bottle of Clorox in the other.

"Son, it's not too late to change your mind. You have a good life here. All these new products could be yours. You don't need to do this."

He's sincere, in a strange and belittling way. However, I think he's genuinely going to miss me. My smile offers him sympathy.

"No, Dad, this is it for me. I can't fulfill my destiny here. I don't know what I'm going to do, but I know I'll be happy."

I watch as my family disappears behind the front door. With a pocket full of money and overzealous confidence, I feel ready to do anything. Nashville, here I come.

WEEKDAY

Every morning at 7 a.m., a loud siren jolts me out of a nightmare and into a new one. With half an hour to get ready, I stumble to the kitchen and pour myself a cup of inspiration. It should last me till noon. I wash myself of yesterday's pain, then rush downstairs in hopes of snagging at least a pop tart before I leave. In a perfect rhythm, my wife slips a wad of foil into my hand and a small Hydro Flask. I take a peek into the foil.

Turkey sausage and egg whites on an English muffin. Bless this woman.

I rush out the door for work. Having left the comfort of my home, I'm soon comforted by NPR as Sam Sanders cancels out the American noise of bumper-to-bumper traffic. Just as I start to enjoy my time alone, anxiety convinces me that I'll be late for work. I check for my estimated arrival time and race the GPS. As usual, I make it to work with thirty seconds to spare. I slip into my cubicle unnoticed. I work as a financial advisor and have the pleasure of helping low-income families surf the poverty line. After disappointing my first client of the day, I immediately crave a break. It has been exactly three hours since I had coffee. It's time for a refill.

I muddle through several hours of empty advice until I'm released at 4:30 p.m. I unhook the chains connecting my ankles to the desk, clear my station, and free myself from the cubicle. I rush past customers and run towards my car. While I look like a man excited to run home to his wife and kids, I'm actually a man running anxiously towards somebody's dollar menu. But if I stop somewhere, I'll have to get the kids something too. Never mind, we have food at home.

I rush off in order to avoid traffic. After arriving at my house in record time, I'm greeted by two overly hyper children eager to leave for soccer and cheerleading practice. And ding ding ding, you've guessed it. I'm the one taking them. I question why I've rushed home just to clock in for another job. With no break to eat or rest, I snap on my driver's cap and steer my life into autopilot. The kids and I hit the road just in time for the thick of traffic. I spend the majority of the ride reassuring my son Tanner that he's perfectly capable of scoring goals without me sitting in a lawn chair holding his water bottle. With great reluctance, he complies, and Lily and I set off to her cheer studio. With Tanner and Lily in the hands of someone else for two hours, I take a long, deserved nap.

Thirty seconds later, I awake to four messages on my phone. One from my son's coach, and three from my daughter's studio. A bit over the top, but that's cheer-leading. Both of their practices have been over for an hour. It's 9:30 p.m. I curse to myself and quickly race to grab the kids.

I receive a lengthy lecture from both coaches as I've made them wait with my kids, again. As their scolding treads on, I can't help but think we could all be in bed right now. On the drive back home, I seriously contemplate my life. I'm tired of taking the kids to practice. I'm tired of working eight hours just to work another four after. I'm tired of fueling my days with liquid just to burn out halfway through the day. I'm tired of wasting my financial expertise on the financially illiterate. Each day is clouded with a plethora of tasks; I've forgotten what a break feels like. Heck, I don't even remember how to spell it. Why should I have to struggle while my wife sits at home twiddling her thumbs? She always complains about slaving over a stove, but I'm slaving over a steering wheel playing chauffeur. By the way, if she puts that much effort into cooking, why is her chicken always dry? Okay, that's unfair. Her baked chicken is actually delightful. However, I don't take back what I said about needing a break. I'm really tired.

With my energy lavishly spent, I drowsily rally the kids into bed. As I quietly enter the master bedroom, I see my wife sound asleep on her side of the bed. I face plant onto the queen-sized mattress and release a tired sigh. My wife stirs awake and rolls over to kiss me.

"Hey, babe?"

I roll around to face her and brace myself for an assignment or an early morning errand.

"Yes, honey?"

"Thank you."

I smile.

"You're welcome. I love you."

"Love you too."

BRAND NEW FRIEND

Oatmeal a day keeps the pimples away. But because oatmeal is a time teaser, Kelley settles for the cucumber exfoliator instead. She squeezes a dollop onto her palm and rubs vigorously. It's already the second week, and the cleanser has proved no visible results. But there's a slight brightening of her overall tone as the packaging promised. She went from a blonde roast to a caramel macchiato. She curses to herself as she remembers her roommate used the last of their cucumber moisturizer.

"Darn it, Danny."

With no other alternative, she spreads a thin layer of Vaseline over her cheeks. Quickly glancing down at her phone, she sees it's already 7:35 a.m. She sprints – *briskly walks* – out the front door towards her car with keys and a protein bar riding safely under her arm. In a panic, she speeds through Highway 41 – *three miles over the speed limit* – and prays the highway patrolman is on a doughnut run.

As she enters the office building, her eyes dart towards the analog clock.

"*Yes,* eight forty-five on the dot," she says with an overweening smirk on her face. She strolls blissfully through the building with mischievous eyes like she knows something her co-workers don't.

Work starts at 9:00 a.m., but Kelley always shows up early to make sure nothing goes on without her knowing. She gives small and quick greetings to her office mates before slipping quietly into her double-doored office. It's arguably the largest space in the building. She sits at her white, large-scale wooden table. Atop her desk is a single bamboo plant, a picture of her parents, and an inappropriately large desktop. She begins to type away the day, comforted in writer's bliss. Her office has floor to ceiling glass walls that offer her both a door for conversation and a door for solitude, the best of both worlds. She loves the peace and lack of conversation it brings. Her mantra: *Why talk to people when candles are a thing?*

Kelley is the only content writer with their own office. Due to her boss's recent rebranding/firing spree, she inherited her own miniature paradise. As she works through pages of editing, she can't help but dread the inevitable interruption of her sweet silence. It's quiet. Too quiet. And her imagined spidey sense always detects human activity accurately. As she pokes her head from the side of her large computer, two figures appear outside her door. Her boss, Brock, is a tall, slim man wrapped in an even slimmer grey suit. By his side stands a fair-skinned woman with a clever smile. This girl is unfamiliar to Kelley.

"Good morning, Kelley, I'd love for you to meet our new lead photographer, Cody. I'm partnering you guys up for the upcoming newsletter, so you two will be working together for the next few months or so. Oh, and by the way. She's your uh...new officemate. Bye!"

He quickly leaves to avoid any objecting parties. Cody then enters the office offering a warm smile. Kelley responds with the same. She then takes a seat across from Kelley and lets out an audible sigh of relief.

"This office is really beautiful; there's so much light."

"Thank you. I figured it'd be difficult to write in the dark. So, let there be light."

She lets out a small chuckle. Kelley is surprised. She anticipated an eye roll, an eyebrow lift, or maybe even a condescending smirk. But not a laugh.

"So, what's it like around here?"

"What's it like?"

"Yea, what's the vibe of the office? Do you guys listen to music or have Taco Tuesdays?"

"No tacos, but Paul's having a party after work tomorrow."

"Really? That could be really fun. Are you going?"

"I don't really care for the extracurriculars. But you should go."

"Hmm... I think I will. So, how long have you been working here?"

"I scored an internship with Fairy Trail straight out

of college and was promoted to lead writer after one year. Today actually marks my fourth year as Executive Content Writer."

"Wow, congratulations, you moved forward at a startup company. That's impressive. You must be pretty amazing."

"Thanks." A curt response to hide her inner satisfaction. Kelley smirks before reverting her attention to her work. It's about time people start to recognize her rare expertise. *Extra brownie points for Cody for giving honor where honor is due.*

"So, I guess I'll be running my photos by you for the website. Should I call you Miss Kelley?"

"Whatever works. Just don't call me late for dinner!"

She didn't earn a laugh and was instantly embarrassed by the lame response. She has never said that in her life, but at that moment, it flew out.

A few minutes pass by and Cody subtly asks, "Why does it smell so good in here!"

What Cody smells is the decadent aroma of fresh linen. Kelley swears by her fresh linen-scented candles. If anyone complains of lack of sleep or marital issues, she would simply prescribe them one of those three-wick wonders.

"It's one of my candles from home. I hope you don't mind the smell."

"Not at all, I live for candles – who doesn't gleam at the smell of a clean shirt?"

Kelley abruptly stops typing and grows taller in her seat. *Yes! Exactly!* Kelley and Cody share a small smile and then continue to work.

Okay, she can stay.

"After four years of blissful solitude, I'm being forced to share my space," Kelley explains to Danny as he makes his infamous grilled sushi. A thick smell of raw fish fills the apartment. "I guess it was only a matter of time. And she seems cooperative. She liked my candle."

"She? She who?"

"Cody, her name is Cody. She was very friendly. The kind of friendliness that makes you think they know something you don't."

Focused on the sushi, he holds the bamboo mat in position, applying pressure to the roll with his fingers, and lines the salmon towards the end of the nori.

"Oh, Cody's a cool name."

"Keep up, Danny. I'm worried about who this girl is! What if she's a covert agent, or what if she starts to bring egg rolls for lunch? You know I hate eggs, especially when rolled. Or what if she's my replacement?

"How often do they replace writers with photographers?"

Kelley sinks deeper into the couch and sighs in frustration. Danny jumps over the couch and plops down next to her. "Kelley, I know you don't want to hear this, but you're overreacting. I think this could be good for you. Just the other day you were complaining about not having anyone else to talk to besides me. So, here's your opportunity. Make a friend."

Danny takes a large bite into the grilled sushi and smiles warmly at her. His phone buzzes.

"All right, ladies and gentlemen, Becca will be here in five minutes. So, if you are not my date, we ask that you exit the space."

Danny peels Kelley off the couch and directs her into her room. She face-plants onto her bed and contemplates her fate with Cody. Perhaps this office arrangement could be the start of something new.

Kelley shimmies through a group of tipsy coworkers and a thick cloud of barbecue and bourbon. She scans the room for a corner to call her own.

Kelley doesn't have a good reason for being at this party. She also has no reason to stay home. She very well couldn't let the new girl attend her first work party alone. Paul has had his birthday extravaganza at the Blue Moon Cafe for three years in a row. And every year, he begs Kelley to join him on stage to sing 'Total Eclipse of the Heart.' And every year, she hides by the bar until he finds someone else. Kelley likes Paul but hates the spotlight more.

Far off, Kelley hears yells and cheers coming from the stage. Paul is on his fourth song blowing through Michael Bolton's best hits when he starts to become hysterical, screaming without a cause. He's about two or three sheets to the wind and three seconds away from sliding off the stage. She figures she should step in before he hurts himself. Kelley swoops in towards the stage and collects Paul. She gently slings his arm over her shoulders and holds him up with her other hand. He is surprisingly compliant and obedient. With little murmuring or complaining, Kelley guides Paul to a seat at the bar next to her.

"I'll have a –" Paul begins to order before Kelley quickly interjects.

"Water. He'll have water."

Paul crosses his arms and sips reluctantly through the bendy straw.

"I think we've had enough drinking and karaoke for the night."

Just as the words leave her mouth, her eyes shoot to the stage to see Cody shaking her hips to 'Party in the USA' with a drink in one hand and a mic in the other.

It's getting late, so Kelley takes a seat conveniently close to the exit. After a thrilling performance, Cody scans the cafe for any duet partners. After what feels like five minutes of searching, Cody locks eyes with Kelley. Kelley quickly turns her head back down to her phone. She now realizes that it's time to go. Kelley shoves her debit card into her purse and bolts faster than you can say, "Social anxiety." As her hand just barely grasps the handle of the door, she hears Cody's voice boom from the stage.

"Is that Kelley over there? OMG! Get up here! Everyone, give it up for Kelley!"

All eyes cut to Kelley. She hasn't been this embarrassed since she brought a casserole dish to a dorm room hangout. They begin to cheer, ushering her to join Cody onstage. Kelley blushes deeply under the overwhelming attention. Before she can protest, Kelley finds herself walking bravely towards the stage. She plans to have a stern talk with her legs on the way back home. Kelley grabs a mic and looks at Cody with panicky eyes. At this moment, she hates Cody for inviting her up. But she hates herself even more for accepting.

"Don't worry, we'll do this together. I've got the perfect song for us."

'Dancing Queen' pours loudly from the speakers. Kelley's eyes light up. Although she's never been much of a performer, she can't hide her love for this timeless track. *Mamma Mia!* is her absolute favorite musical. Kelley knows all the lyrics, and to her surprise, so does Cody! Neither of them takes a single glance at the lyric screen.

Kelley looks thoughtfully at Cody and is enamored. She is a natural entertainer. Within the first five minutes, she has everyone on their feet singing along. She has the personality that could make you feel comfortable in the most uncomfortable circumstance. Being the center of attention seems to fall naturally on her shoulders. She knows exactly what to do with it. On the other hand, Kelley hates extended attention and finds it overwhelming. But tonight, she feels freer than she ever has before. What once was uncomfortable has become the most exhilarating feeling in the world.

Their short set turns into an hour of singing. Cody has an insane ability to make time move slower.

Kelley and Cody begin to hang out more often. Almost every day after work, the two and maybe a few others from the office would head to the Punch Bowl for drinks and bowling. Punch Bowl is their favorite because, after 10 p.m., the tacos are half off. For the first time since college, Kelley is leaving the house for more than just almond butter and French dip. She actually has plans. Although she prefers being at home, she loves Cody's company.

Kelley slips out of her room wearing white dress shorts, a sequined camisole, and a white blazer. Perfectly polished.

"We're freshly stocked with groceries – why are you leaving the house?"

"Shut up, I go places. I do things."

"Yes, for about forty-five minutes, then you come home and roll into a ball."

"I have plans with my friend Cody."

"Again? I'm impressed. Three weeks in, and you've already tricked her into being your friend."

Kelley rolls her eyes, clipping her earrings on and slipping into her pink suede Tory Burch loafers.

"I took your advice. Cody is actually really awesome. She likes musicals and is obsessed with the winter candle line from Bath & Body Works. She likes candles, Danny."

"Still…don't tunnel vision. You do that a lot."

Kelley brushes his words off, and they share a quick smile. He shouts, "Have fun" before she shuts the door behind her.

Finding a friend is like finding a good shampoo; once you find one that works, the search is over. There is no need to fish for more once you've found your person. And Kelley has finally found her person. Cody is an all-in-one package. She's funny, relatable, authentic, and sensitive. And a terrific listener. She's the only friend Kelley needs.

Monday morning arrives, and everyone is in their respective offices working. It's only 9:30 and Kelley is already knee-deep in her third page of editing. The new pages she's assigned to edit for the website feature gorgeous pictures by the amazingly talented Cody Carson. Cody's photography is nothing short of perfection. She's easy to get along with and good at her job. A rare find.

"Cody, these pictures are so hot. You did a great job."

"Thanks. Mason made the shoot fly by. He's so natural in front of the camera."

Mason walks through the door, a dark-skinned man with bushy brown hair, and golden eyes that were both playful and cold. He gives Cody a peck on the lips. Without lingering for a moment, he turns his attention to Kelley, giving her a nod. Kelley eyes his body with intense curiosity. Cody and Mason stand within an inch of each other, leaving no room for Jesus. She can't look away. Mason is not only photogenic but life-genic.

"Oh yeah, Kellogs, speaking of the hot devil himself, meet Mason."

"The pleasure's all mine." Mason extends his hand.

"All mine, actually." She shakes his weakly.

Kelley can't decide which is stranger: Cody's new office fling or the fact that she's been christened "Kellogs." After a few minutes of small talk, Mason kisses Cody goodbye and sets off to do whatever beautiful people do in the afternoon.

As soon as the two girls are alone, Kelley can't help but search for details. "When were you gonna tell me that you were seeing a model?"

Cody blushes hard. "I know, I know. It kinda just happened out of nowhere. After our shoot last week, he asked me out. And guess what, Kelley?"

"What?"

"I said yes."

"You're kidding." A bit sarcastic.

Both of them laugh at the juvenility of their situation. Kelley can't help but feel happy for her; she's a sucker for organic romance.

"Bad news though, Mason bought tickets to this hockey game. So, I might need a raincheck on drinks."

"No problem. Have fun with your man. We'll hang out some other time."

"You're the best, Kelster!" Cody smiles.

"How do you come up with these?"

Brock storms into the room distressed and lays himself on Kelley's office chair.

"Kelley…" He smiles like he needs a huge favor.

"What do you need, Brock?"

"I know it's Friday, but there's a new opportunity to launch a promo video for our special feature on the app. If you're interested, the videographer needs a clean script, voice-over, and good photos. Maybe you and Cody could collaborate?"

"That's if I can track her down. She's been out of the office a lot lately."

"If this is too late notice…"

"No, Brock, we can do this. Trust me."

"That's what I like to hear. I need it uploaded by Monday morning."

Kelley felt this is the perfect project to bring them back together, to reunite the fearsome twosome, the ultimate duo, the fabulous females. Cody has always talked about working on a new and exciting project – Kelley is sure this would excite her.

The sun rises on a beautiful Saturday morning, and Kelley is hunched over her MacBook with three cups of old tea scattered across her desk. She's been up since 5 a.m., writing the script and recording the voiceover. The couple living above her apartment gets very vocal at night, which ruined a couple of takes. Once the final piece is done, she'd be able to send the material to the video editor. All that's left are stunning photos from Cody, which Kelley knows she's capable of.

However, she hasn't been able to reach her all Saturday. Deciding to take a small break, Kelley logs into Instagram. She taps on Cody's story, and the beautiful architecture of the Palace of Fine Arts covers her iPhone X screen. *She's in SF? That must be why she's missed my calls.*

Kelley sees Mason standing proudly at the top of a staircase. Before she can finish the video, she throws the iPhone against her pillow. Just then, it beeps.

Cody: Hey, Kelley, sorry can't talk I'm in SF

Kelley can't believe it. She needs Cody's photos to complete this project before Monday. There's no one else who can do it as well as her. Cody will come through, Kelley is absolutely sure of it. As long as she knows how much it means to her.

Kelley: I saw on IG! SF has beautiful architecture. Is there any way you could snap a couple of photos, run them through photoshop, and send them to me? This project is time-sensitive.

Kelley waits by the phone for a response that never comes. After a long hour of convincing another photographer to help out, Kelley is able to upload the promo. Monday morning comes sooner than desired. Kelley tiredly crawls to her office. To her surprise, Cody is already there.

"Have you had a sushirrito? It's from a place in SF where they fuse sushi with burritos."

"I haven't had the chance, but it does sound interesting. The pictures on IG looked great."

"You saw my story? Yeah, Mason was so excited. You know, he's never seen a professional musical production? We're thinking of staying the weekend with some of his friends next time and seeing *Mean Girls*."

"I thought we were gonna see that together."

The words spill out before she can process them. She aims to remain cool and composed. They stare for a second.

"I know we talked about it, but we never planned anything."

"Sure." Void of emotion. "So, you like Mason, huh?"

"He's a lot of fun. I love experiencing new things with him. He lights up like a little kid. It's weekends like this that make me want to explore the world. It's so much bigger than California. I don't see how someone could live in one place their entire life."

"California's warm."

For the rest of the workday, the office is quiet. Kelley and Cody work until the day is done. They leave with polite goodbyes.

The clock strikes one and the break room crowds like a cafeteria. Before Kelley can bite into her turkey pesto sandwich, she hears Cody's voice blaring.

"Friday night at seven is game night at my house! I'll text the address!"

Cody takes a seat next to Kelley and steals a few of her chips.

"Game night?" Kelley inquires.

"Yes! Cards Against Humanity, Twister, and glow in the dark Mafia!"

"Exciting stuff," Kelley comments, mildly amused.

"Yep! And the best part is that you're on snack duty."

Kelley feels uneasy. "Oh, great," she says unconvincingly.

"Don't overthink it. Just chips and dip. Stuff like that." She takes a few more Doritos from Kelley's plate.

"A little party never killed nobody!"

To Kelley's surprise, their first party went swimmingly. While Kelley isn't typically thrilled by the idea of parties, she took her position as a snack provider very seriously. Her tomato, basil, and bacon flatbread was a huge hit! It's amazing how much better a party can be when you can crowd around the food. The first party went over so well, Cody decides to host another the following week. As the party guests grow in numbers, Kelley's snacks mature into appetizers. People at the office even start acting differently since having the weekly shindigs. They would come up to her and just start to talk, without any prompting. She has become someone people chat with about nothing and it's nice. And it's all thanks to Cody's parties.

Lunch time arrives and the Fairy Trail break room is packed to the brim.

"Kelley, these meatballs are amazing, and I don't even like pork!"

"Thanks, Paul! It's my special sauce. A mix of pineapple, soy sauce, and teriyaki."

"Why haven't you made this for game night? Are you holding out on us?"

"Just practicing. These bad boys will be front and center this weekend."

"I'm so there."

As lunch comes to an end, everyone starts to clear out, leaving Cody and Kelley.

Cody is frustratedly texting on her phone, and Kelley notices.

"You're in a peppy mood," she says sarcastically.

"Sorry, I'm glued to my phone. Mason's been texting me non-stop today."

Kelley tries to hide her face. She's been working hard to like Mason, but Ken dolls don't have much of a personality, just good looks, and tight abs. But she tries, for Cody. But every once in a while, the sound of his name bothers her.

"Kelley…don't hate me."

"What?"

"Mason and I haven't hung out in two weeks and this is the first time our schedules align. I have to cancel game night."

Kelley is silent.

"But what am I apologizing for, you always say canceled plans are more of a relief than a disappointment, right?"

Kelley pokes at meatballs on her plate, drawing circles with the sauce. "Right."

"Raincheck?"

"Of course."

"You're the absolute best, Kelley!"

She leaves and smiles widely, enthralled over whatever Mason is texting. Kelley is left alone. She walks over to the counter and sees four lonely meat balls at the bottom of the pan. She roughly throws the pan into the wastebasket. Sure, Kelley would have brushed it off if it were anybody else's party. But Cody isn't just anybody. Her presence is unmistakable, and becoming more and more necessary in her life. Cody understands Kelley like nobody at the office ever attempted to. Canceled plans with Cody are never a relief, only a disappointment.

Unfortunately, game night takes more than a single week off. When Cody's relationship with Mason heats up, the parties cool down, as do her interactions with Kelley. They aren't as close, yet not fully estranged either. Their weekly drinks slow to monthly check-ins via text.

"Kelley, you have to bring that flatbread tomorrow night." Paul beamed.

"For what?"

"Cody's party."

Kelley's heart dropped. Cody's party? How is she the last to know about this? "Cody hasn't had a party in weeks," she said.

"Oh, I thought I heard Lily mention a party at Cody's last week. Maybe I misheard. I'm sure your office mate can fill you in."

Kelley is mortified. Had Cody been hosting game nights without her? Why? Maybe Paul didn't know what he was talking about.

Later that week, when Friday arrives, the idea of being excluded from multiple game nights continues to weigh on her mind. Kelley tries to talk herself out of the negativity.

She's not mad at me or anything. We were having such a great time. There's no way she'd forget to invite me. We're friends. I ought to check in with her. That's what friends do, right? I have her address. I could always just drop by.

After dropping off books at the library, she recognizes the neighborhood. Cody lives a few miles from here. It is half-past six. About the time she'd be heading to Cody's place—if there was a party tonight. Which there's not. Because Cody would never purposely exclude her best friend from a game night. But just to make sure, she figures she might as well swing by and take a peek.

Kelley cancels the address in the GPS and types in Cody's.

I'm in the neighborhood. It only makes sense. Maybe we'll end up watching a movie or something.

After a fifteen-minute drive, Kelley pulls up and parks across the street from Cody's house. Cody's 2019 Nissan Versa is parked in the driveway.

She's home.

But there's another car—*she doesn't recognize it.* It's parked on the curb out front. Unless Cody's recently bought another car, she has company. Mason, she assumes.

So, it's clear there's no party going on, which is a relief. But she drove all this way; it feels silly to leave so soon. And of course, it would be rude to invite herself in when Cody's entertaining. She takes out her phone and turns on the camera app. She figures, if she can see for herself that it's just Mason in there, she can rest easy. She zooms in close—the camera on the iPhone X is phenomenal. And there they are, sitting on the couch together. *All right, nothing to see there.* But something catches her eye.

Is that my black widow-themed potholder?

She leans over to get a better look. Her elbow slips and her chin smashes into the steering wheel. A loud horn blares.

Oh, shoot.

She sees a finger peer through the curtain towards the street. She tosses her phone in the passenger seat and sinks to hide herself.

I shouldn't be here.

Crouched down, she inches her key into the ignition—her heart racing. As she speeds through the neighborhood, her stomach twists in a pang of discomfort. She feels like puking.

What am I doing?

Kelley walks lazily through the kitchen, tucking a jar of almond butter and a pack of Oreos under her arms, then heads to her bedroom. She hears a gentle knock on the door. Danny enters to find Kelley slumped on her bed flipping through Korean dramas on Netflix.

"Hey, did you finish the Oreos?"

"Hold on."

Kelley roughly dips the last cookie into the jar of almond butter, then launches it into her mouth. She sighs in satisfaction. "Yes. I'll get more tomorrow."

Danny climbs onto the sheets and lays himself across the end.

"You're home later than usual. Out with your bestie again?"

"I was at the Cheesecake Factory stuffing myself with cake. Cody's been busy."

He picks up a nail buffer and begins shining his nails.

"I listen better with smooth nail buds," he says. "Everything good between you two?"

"Peachy."

He shows her his finished thumb, perfectly polished. Kelley is impressed at the speed.

"It's funny when Cody started working at Fairy Trail, work became exciting. I actually went out after work with coworkers. She made work fun. Being around her was exciting. I guess I feel like, without her, I'm just—plain."

"Come on, Kelley, you're not plain. You're exciting!"

"I spent half my paycheck on candles and pot-holders."

"Sure, you shop like an old lady. But hey, old ladies are exciting too."

"I don't know, I can't shake the feeling that she's getting bored with me."

"Cody seems like the type that likes a variety. I wouldn't worry about your friendship. Plus, the relationship is new. The last time I had a girlfriend, you didn't hear from me for months!"

"So, you're saying it may be months before I hear from her?"

"I'm saying you're overthinking it. She's just learning how to balance her new boyfriend and her friends. It's nothing personal. She's in the honeymoon phase. It'll wear off soon."

Kelley doesn't want to admit it, but Danny has a point. Maybe she has nothing to do with their thinning relationship. Maybe it isn't that Cody doesn't want to hang with her, but that she wants to hang out with her boyfriend more.

Kelley is wearisome of the direction of things. But, friendships change, and every long-lasting friendship evolves. If Cody and Kelley's friendship is to last, it would have to muddle through some light turbulence.

A few weeks go by, and the distance between Cody and Kelley grows larger. After getting a new opportunity at a competing company, they hardly see each other. They've exchanged only a few texts since their departure. She'd tag Cody in a Facebook meme, Cody would like it, and that was the extent of their interaction.

One bright Sunday afternoon, Kelley strolls down the frozen section at Trader Joe's. Danny usually handled the grocery shopping, as the activity of scavenging around a crowded room searching for items annoyed her. But he insisted she leave the house at least once this week. And besides, French dip doesn't grow on trees.

While searching aisle by aisle for some paprika, Kelley spots a familiar blondie reaching for a box of Bran Flakes. Her heart shifts—Immediately unsettled. Seeing someone you know at a store is a social night-mare in which Kelley is intimately familiar. If it were anybody else, Kelley would bolt from the aisle, abandoning the paprika mission altogether. But *this* is a close-friend.

"Cody?"

She says brightly, as if she hadn't spotted her twenty-seconds ago.

Cody turns around to see Kelley with an assuring grin on her face.

"Oh wow, Kelley!" Her voice is loud enough to be heard from many aisles down.

The two quickly embrace.

"It feels like it's been forever! How have you been?" Kelley asks.

"Good. Work's been keeping me busy. How 'bout you?"

"Same. I took on a bit more responsibility when you transferred, but I'm managing well. How's Mason doing?"

"Uh, we stopped seeing each other a while back." Kelley's voice is now a bit softer. She shrugs casually.

"Aww, man."

"We had our fun. It was time to move on. What about you, are you dating anyone?"

"No. I guess guys aren't in the market for awkward, introverted workaholics."

They share a brief laugh. It feels like the interaction is ending soon. Kelley panics. Like a tea kettle on the verge of boiling over, she blurts out, "We should grab drinks soon. Maybe have a girls' night?" She's pleading more than suggesting.

Cody loads for a moment before responding, "Yeah, maybe."

"This might be too fast, but are you free tonight?"

"I love your eagerness, but tonight's no good."

"Oh, well, what does your weekend look like?"

"Work, mostly. Maybe we can just leave it up in the air."

"I don't know, we're not so great at leaving plans up in the air. They usually just evaporate."

They laugh.

Cody confesses lightly, "This is nice. I like talking to you every once in a while when it's natural. Like right now."

"This is just running into me at the grocery store. You just want to run into me?"

"No, I just don't think we need to force anything."

"I don't think it's forceful to make plans. We haven't hung out in three months."

Irritated, Cody drops the bran cereal into her cart. All subtleties removed.

"Okay, well, what do you wanna talk about? You go to work, go home, and you don't have a boyfriend. It doesn't take long to catch up with you. What else is there?"

Taken aback, Kelley is dumbstruck. Her body tightens as emerging tears constrict her throat. The reality of the situation hit her like an avalanche.

"You'd know what else there is if you'd take the time to listen. I feel like this is coming out of nowhere."

"I mean… I don't know what you want me to say. It's cool being your friend, but it's just…"

"If it's a time thing, I understand. We can just text, I can give you –"

"I have your number, Kelley."

"Oh, then, we can FaceTime. Or we could do Zoom. I'm open—"

"I just don't want to talk to you!" Cody blurts out, turning the heads of nearby customers.

A moment of silence falls between them.

"I'm sorry, Kelley, but maybe you need to hear this. I don't want to stay in contact with you, I don't want updates, I don't want texts, I just wanna be done. You're not a fun person to be around. I like spontaneity, trying new things. And you order the same thing from Starbucks every week. I want to go out at night without feeling like I'm babysitting a Make-A-Wish kid. You're a nice person, but I'm done entertaining."

At a loss for words, Kelley stands with her jaw low enough to scrape the bottom of the earth. After a painful minute, Cody grips her cart and pushes towards the checkout.

Kelley remains, feeling cold and embarrassed. She's racking her brain for what she'd done to make Cody so upset. They had had so much fun at Fairy Trail. So many office parties and game nights. They sang ABBA together. Was it all just smoke and mirrors? Was it all just a chore for her? Nothing made sense. How could you be so close with somebody and then just throw them away?

Realizing she's been blocking the bran cereal for the last fifteen minutes, Kelley finally comes out of her trauma and heads towards checkout. She decides to leave without the paprika.

She drags her cart to checkout lane three and waits. She replays the scene repeatedly in her head, ruminating over her humiliation.

You're not a fun person to be around.

I just wanna be done.

Kelley questions whether she was ever a good friend to Cody.

Was I smothering her? If I was, why didn't she say something? I can adjust and adapt. That's what relationships are about: compromise. If I'd known I needed to change around her, I would have changed. I just needed direction.

If she knew that I could change, maybe things would be different. If I could have a minute to explain. If we could just grab a coffee, I could apologize and all of this misunderstanding would be cleared up. I'm not sure, but I think she might need some time. I could call in a week.

Kelley can see Cody already checked out heading towards the exit. As the automatic slide doors open for Cody, the girls lock eyes for a moment. Cody's straight and emotionless. One look and Kelley is reminded of all the pain endured from Cody's words. Kelley looks to the ground as her eyes begin to water.

What has happened to me? What am I even doing?

Engulfed in the realization that her friend is a thing of the past, Kelly's mind is woefully made up. She pays for her groceries and heads towards her car. As Kelley enters the comfort of her driver's seat, she immediately retrieves her phone from her pocket. Scrolling through her contacts, she finds Cody's name.

I can't call her.

Kelly deletes Cody's number then slides her key into the ignition.

I need to be done too.

YOU ARE NEXT RODRIGUEZ
Stephen King | On Writing |
Redeeming Love FRANCINE RIVERS
Do Not Become Alarmed MAILE MELOY

SAMARIA

Samaria Sylvester is a social introvert on a mission to build connections while still leaving the party early. Having been born in Misawa, Japan, and driven across the States as an Air Force brat, being the new kid (especially the new black kid), is basically her lifestyle. Foreign environments make her feel most at home. While her writing interests battle for her attention, consuming her daily thoughts, her desire to add hope to those around her and be what her loved ones need remains at the top of her priority list. When she's not frantically jotting down a story idea, hoping the thought won't pass, or belting Dear Evan Hansen at the top of her lungs, she enjoys playing piano, leading worship at a women's prayer group, and impromptu movie nights with her dad and brother.

Her favorite genres are humor, young adult, adventure, and psychological thrillers. Her fascination with human behavior and personality nuances greatly influence her voice and style. Sylvester resides in Sacramento, California, with her mother, father, and brother.

YOU ARE NEXT
RODRIGUEZ
Stephen King | On Writing |
Redeeming Love
FRANCINE RIVERS

MICHAEL

Michael Sylvester is a writer of both comedies and dramas for young adults. He was born in Misawa, Japan, and spent many years of his childhood traveling as a military dependent. In addition to writing short stories, Michael is a passionate videographer, musician, and home chef. Regardless of the pastime, he prides himself in being someone to call when you need a good friend or a good cookie.